THE TWELVE CATS OF CHRISTMAS

For Jonny and Fran - AR
For Ámbar and Niam - MM

SIMON & SCHUSTER
First published in Great Britain in 2020 by Simon & Schuster UK Ltd
1st Floor, 222 Gray's Inn Road, London, WC1X 8HB
Text copyright © 2020 Alison Ritchie • Illustrations copyright © 2020 Marisa Morea
The right of Alison Ritchie and Marisa Morea to be identified as the author and illustrator of this work
has been asserted by them in accordance with the Copyright, Designs and Patents Act, 1988
All rights reserved, including the right of reproduction in whole or in part in any form
A CIP catalogue record for this book is available from the British Library upon request
978-1-4711-9118-3 (PB) • 978-1-4711-9117-6 (eBook)
Printed in Great Britain by Bell & Bain Ltd, Glasgow • 10 9 8 7 6 5 4 3 2

THE TWELVE CATS OF CHRISTMAS

Alison Ritchie and Marisa Morea

SIMON & SCHUSTER

London   New York   Sydney   Toronto   New Delhi

It's Christmas and the cheeky cats are counting down the days.

There's so much festive fun to have,
in so many different ways!

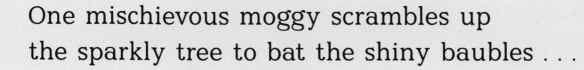

One mischievous moggy scrambles up
the sparkly tree to bat the shiny baubles . . .

and catch a
mouse for tea.

Two tangled tabbies are all tied up with string –

wrapping Christmas presents is definitely not their thing!

Three merry marmalades make their Christmas wish –

that Santa Claus will bring them a yummy piece of fish.

Four peaceful Persians are comfy sleepyheads,
purring all day long in their cosy Christmas beds!

Who will be the first to find the turkey's hiding place?

Six musical moggies are full of Christmas cheer

as they caterwaul their carols for EVERYONE to hear!

Seven sourpusses kitted out in reindeer hats

are pretty sure that fancy dress is NOT cool for cats!

Eight athletic alley cats have
nearly reached their prize . . .

Lost dog

an enormous
Christmas pudding –
right before their eyes!

Nine curious kittens are on a special Christmas quest
to unwrap all the gifts to see which one's the best!

Ten brave bobcats
sledge down a hill too steep . . .

Twelve pacing pussycats on the rooftops way up high
watch eagerly for Santa and his reindeer to come by.

And as the night sky fills with
the jingle of Santa's sleigh,

ALL the cheeky cats wish you . . .

. . . a **purrfect** Christmas Day!